A PARTY
FOR ARTIE

Written by Cathy Blanck
Illustrated by Sarah Marino

Special Thanks to Thom Blanck
and Melissa Nguyen

Dedicated to all of the racehorses
who are given a second chance.

Arctic Course or Artie, as his friend Ariel calls him, is a horse who just moved to Runaround Farm.

"Hurry up Artie! You can win!" she yelled laughing. Ariel knew he was pretending to race another horse, remembering the real races he had won over the years.

"You're almost to the finish line!" Ariel cheered over her shoulder as she walked into the barn to greet her friends, the other farm animals.

"Hi everyone, I'm so glad to see you!" bubbled Ariel as she quickly passed out invitations to a welcome party for Artie.

"A party, what fun!" squealed Pretty Pig and her sister Wilma.

"Yes!" exclaimed Ariel. "I'm glad you are all excited because this is important to me. I want to make Artie feel just as loved here, in his new home, as he felt in his old home. I will bake him a big carrot cake and some other goodies. I know he likes to eat, but I am not sure what gift to give him. Any ideas?" Ariel asked hopefully.

The cows hung their heads in a thoughtful way. The goats casually chewed while pondering this. Pretty Pig and Wilma discussed how it would be hard to find a gift for someone they did not know too well. The animals sat and thought about gifts for a while until one by one they went back to their pastures, rafters and pens to start planning.

The entire farm yard was buzzing with excitement because the big day was finally here. All of the farm animals gathered in the barn just as the invitation directed.

"Good morning," greeted Ariel. "Just look at all of the beautiful gifts. Artie will be so happy."

As the bright, warm sun peeked through the cracks of the barn, Artie awoke. He stood up, stretched his long legs and gave a huge yawn.

"Oh no!" exclaimed Artie, "I must have over slept. I'm sure all of the other animals are outside already."

He quickly trotted out of his stall, down the long aisle way and pulled open the heavy barn doors.

"SURPRISE ARTIE!" shouted Ariel and the animals.

"We wanted to give you a warm, friendly welcome to Runaround Farm," said Ariel.

They all smiled and huddled around Artie.

Callie, the barn cat, was the first to give her gift.

"I have watched how the Ferrier comes to file down your hooves. I made you a scratching post from an old beam, so you can file your feet anytime you wish just like me," she purred.

The spiders, Ernie and Floyd, who live above Artie's stall, had a very unique gift to give.

"We noticed that when Ariel gives you grain each day you are so happy. You let out a high pitched nicker and go running through your hay. Floyd and I decided to spin a huge net to hang on the wall. This will help to keep your hay in one neat spot," said Ernie.

Next, was the swallow family who live in the wooden rafters at the top of the barn.

"Every morning and evening we watch you walk from the barn to the pasture. It takes you a while to go from your stall, across the lawn and into the field. We thought it would be easier if you could fly. Behind the tractor we found some paper, glue, and string to build you your own set of wings," sang Mother swallow.

After the barn swallows tied on Artie's wings, the pigs dragged over their lovely box tied with rope.

"We sit in our mud pits all day and never worry about flies biting our tough skin. Then, we see how you constantly swish your tail to keep the flies from biting you. Our mud is so wonderful we wanted to give you some. This will help keep those pesky flies away," squealed Wilma.

Ping, and the other ducks, sat quietly until it was their turn.

"Artie, we know you will love our gift," quacked Ping. "During the day you play so hard in the field that we are certain you're very tired by nightfall. We found an old grain sack and collected some soft feathers to make you your very own pillow. It's just like ours, so we know you will be comfortable."

The goats were finally ready to give their gift.

"Isn't it strange Artie, that when you have an itch to scratch, you have to rub up and down on a fence or lift your leg high in the air to reach it?" asked Gerta the goat. "We know just what you need, your own set of horns to reach those hard to scratch places. We found two big sticks that would be perfect," she snorted.

The cows moseyed over to Artie.

"We sat under the oak trees thinking long and hard for a gift for you Artie," mooed Millie. "Then we realized that because you are new here you could get lost. We found two tin cans and some yarn. Using our creativity, we made a bell for your neck, so we can always find you."

"Thank you everyone! Each of you have made me feel so welcome with your kindness and generous hospitality. This was so thoughtful," sighed Artie.

Artie had a wonderful time at the party. With all the excitement he noticed that he hadn't thought about the racetrack or racing all day. He was now part of the family at Runaround Farm. He also realized that his new friends worked so hard and cared enough for him to create the perfect gifts, and he loved them all.

Who is Artie?

Arctic Course (Artie), is a bay thoroughbred horse who was born June 9, 1997 in Oxford, Michigan. By the age of two he was traveling to Great Lakes Downs in Muskegon, Michigan and racing at the track. Artie loved to race and took the sport very seriously. He had a recognizable face at Great Lakes Downs; some may have even called him a favorite. During his racing career, he had five wins earning over $70,000.00 in purse money. After three years of racing in Michigan, Artie suffered an injury at a track in Chicago, Illinois which caused bone chips in both front knees. Sadly, the injury put an end to Artie's racing life but opened the door to another life.

Artie was donated to the Communication Alliance to Network Thoroughbred Ex-Racehorses Organization (CANTER) by his original owner. CANTER is an organization that places ex-racehorses from the track up for adoption and into loving homes across the United States. They also make sure each of their injured horses are treated before they are ready for placement. Artie received his knee surgery at Michigam State University College of Veterinary Medicine (MSU). Ariel found Artie through CANTER and adopted him in April of 2003.

Artie now resides at a farm in Zeeland, Michigan. There he spends his days running through the pastures, playing with the other horses and learning how to be a wonderful mount. With his amazing work ethic and outstanding athletic ability Artie is now excelling in Dressage. Ariel proudly shows him in Michigan.

A Party for Artie, is a story inspired by an actual event. For Artie's sixth birthday, Ariel threw him a party. She sent out invitations to all of the boarders at the farm, his former owner and jockey, racing trainer, CANTER members, and to MSU. Everyone came to celebrate Artie's birthday. The day included games, food, goodie bags for both the humans and horses, and even gifts. Artie received two fly masks, treats, a halter, and a fly sheet from his guests. This truly was a special day for a very special horse.

The bond between Artie and Ariel is very strong and full of love. Without CANTER the two may have never met. To learn more about CANTER visit www.canterusa.org or e-mail at cantermichigan@canterusa.org . A percentage of the sales from the book *A Party for Artie*, will be donated to CANTER. Thank you for your contribution.